Fairy Ponies

Enchanted Mirror

Zanna Davidson

Illustrated by Barbara Bongini

Meet the Ponies

Holly

Puck

Bluebell

Pony Queen

Princess Rosabel

Spray

Unicorn Prince

Izagard

Shadow

Contents

Chapter One 7

Chapter Two 20

Chapter Three 30

Chapter Four 41

Chapter Five 53

Chapter Six 70

Chapter Seven 81

Chapter One

It was nearing the end of summer vacation
and all Holly could think about were the
amazing adventures she'd had on Pony Island
— a secret world full of fairy ponies, hidden
inside the oak tree at the bottom of her great-
aunt's garden. Tomorrow, Holly would be
going home and leaving Great-Aunt May's
house, and Pony Island, behind her. She had

already said goodbye to her best friend, Puck, the fairy pony, but she couldn't help wishing she could see him again, just one last time.

She climbed into bed, listening to the tap-tapping of branches against her window. But as she lay there, the tapping grew louder, and more insistent.

That's strange, Holly thought. *Maybe the wind is getting stronger?* But when she sat up and looked, she saw a little bird fluttering outside the window, its delicate wings shimmering in the moonlight. Holly knew instantly that it must have come from Pony Island. She tiptoed across the rug-strewn floor and gently opened the window. The bird flew inside and dropped a tiny piece of paper onto her pillow, then swooped out again, disappearing into the night.

Intrigued, Holly bent down to unfurl the paper, which was curled into a miniature scroll. At first, the paper seemed blank, but as she breathed on it, a message appeared in glimmering writing.

Holly, please come to Pony Island as soon as you can. I need your help!

Puck

Holly gasped in surprise. Puck had never sent her a message before. *He must be in trouble!* she thought.

She slipped out of her room, down the stairs and out of the back door. Then she moved swiftly across the moonlit garden until she stood beneath the great oak tree, her heart pounding in her chest. There, she whispered the words of the spell:

"Let me pass into the magic tree,
Where fairy ponies fly wild and free.
Show me the trail of sparkling light,
To Pony Island, shining bright."

As soon as she had finished, Holly slipped her hand into her pocket and pulled out the little bag of magic dust the Pony Queen had given her on her first visit to Pony Island. As she sprinkled it over herself, she felt a tingling in her toes that spread up through her body, and golden sparkles began to dance before her eyes. There was a rush of wind and the next thing Holly knew, she was fairy-sized — small enough to enter the secret tunnel at the bottom of the oak tree. Without pausing for a moment, Holly set off at a run down the passage, following the trail of sparkling light, wanting to reach Puck as quickly as she could.

He was waiting for her at the end of the tunnel, standing knee-deep in the wildflower meadow that marked the beginning of Pony Island.

"Are you all right?" Holly asked breathlessly.
Puck looked the same – his mane and tail
were a burnished brown, and his glossy coat
gleamed in the summer sun – but his
expression was filled with worry.

Puck shook his head, his butterfly wings
fluttering nervously. "Something awful is
happening on Pony Island," he said. "Some of

the fairy ponies are losing their magic."

"Oh no, Puck!" Holly cried. "That's terrible."

"They can't cast spells or even fly," Puck went on. "It all began yesterday, and it seems to be spreading. More and more fairy ponies are saying they've lost their powers, and no one is sure what's causing it."

"What about the Pony Queen and the Spell-Keepers?" asked Holly, thinking of the most powerful and magical ponies on the island. "Do they still have their magic? Can they help?"

"My mom's lost her powers too," said Puck, a tremor in his voice.

"Poor Bluebell," said Holly, stroking Puck's mane. Puck's mother was one of the

Spell-Keepers, and Holly couldn't imagine her not being able to fly.

"The Pony Queen's called an urgent meeting. All the Spell-Keepers are at the palace now. They think it might be some kind of illness."

"I'll do anything I can to help," said Holly. "Where should we start?"

Puck looked determined. "First I want to fly to the Magic Pony Pools in case they can help stop me from losing my powers. All the ponies go there – even the Pony Queen visits once a day for the Royal Bath Time. The pools are a place of healing and well-being, and bathing boosts our powers. Then we could speak to any fairy ponies who have lost their magic, and see if we can find some sort of pattern. What do you think?"

"It's a good plan," Holly agreed. "Let's go."
She leaped onto Puck's back and he took off.

As they flew, Holly glanced around her at
the wildflowers in the meadows and the
gently waving branches of the wooded glades
they passed over. Everywhere seemed oddly
deserted, and Holly wondered if the fairy
ponies were keeping to their homes in fear.

"We're almost there," said Puck, swooping a little lower through the sky. Holly looked down to see the blue, still waters of the Pony Pools.

"Usually the pools are full of Fairy Ponies, playing and bathing," said Puck, as he landed on the soft, grassy ground. "It's strange to see them so empty."

Holly slid off Puck's back and he splashed into the water, until his coat was flecked with spray, shining droplets of water clinging to his mane and tail. "The Magic Pony Pools have amazing healing powers," said Puck. "I always feel better after bathing here, and if there is an illness on the Island, this should help protect me."

After a last canter through the sparkling shallows, Puck came out again, shaking the water from his mane. "I'm ready!" he said, grinning.

"Where should we go first?" asked Holly, climbing onto his back once more.

"There are some huts further along the Singing River," Puck replied. "I heard my mom say some of the ponies there have lost their powers. Let's go and talk to them."

He started forward, beating his wings quickly as he spoke, ready to take to the skies. But his hoofs stayed firmly planted on the ground.

"I don't understand…" Puck began. He beat his wings again and reared up on his hind legs. But still nothing happened.

He moved forward a third time, leaping as hard as he could to try to launch himself into the air, only to land with a heavy thud.

"Oh no!" he gasped. "I can't believe it...I can't fly. I've lost my magic powers too!"

Chapter Two

"Are you sure you've lost your powers?" asked Holly. She swung herself off Puck's back, looking at him with concern. "Why don't you try a spell. How about the drying spell? That's one you know."

"Good idea," said Puck. He cleared his throat, took a deep breath and began to chant the spell:

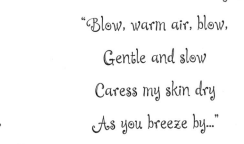

"Blow, warm air, blow,

Gentle and slow

Caress my skin dry

As you breeze by..."

No stirring breeze followed his words. The air stayed still and calm around them, and when Holly reached up to touch Puck's coat, she could feel the water still there, clinging to him like a cloak. "The spell's definitely not working," she said.

"How can I have lost my powers?" cried Puck.

But Holly barely heard him. She was staring out across the Magic Pony Pools, frowning in concentration. "You had your magic powers before you went into the pools..." she said slowly. "And you didn't when you came out. This can only mean one thing, Puck – the Pony Pools have taken away your magic."

Puck snorted and shook his head vehemently. "Everyone goes to the Magic Pony Pools. They *boost* our powers – they don't take them away."

"I don't see what else it can be," said Holly.

"There must be another explanation," insisted Puck.

He tried flapping his wings again, as if he couldn't believe he didn't have the power of flight. But once again, they fluttered uselessly. They stood in silence for a moment, then Puck suddenly stamped his hoofs in surprise. "I've just remembered – I saw my mother on the way to the palace this morning when I went to send you the message. That's when I found out she'd lost her powers too. But she said she'd just been to the Pony Pools."

"That proves it!" said Holly. "It must be more than a coincidence. But what is it about the pools that is making the ponies lose their magic?"

Puck looked dubiously at the crystal clear waters. "I don't know," he said, shaking his head. "They don't look any different. I think the first thing to do is warn the other fairy ponies not to go near the Pony Pools. And we should find out what the Pony Queen and the Spell-Keepers have decided to do."

"That'll take ages if you can't fly," Holly

pointed out gently. "Now we're here, shouldn't we investigate?"

"How?" asked Puck, looking blankly at the waters.

"I think we need to go farther into the Pony Pools," said Holly, thinking hard. "If we can't see anything on the surface, we need to find out what's going on beneath it."

"I don't know, Holly," Puck began. "What if something is in there – I won't be able to use magic to protect us. And I've never been under the water before."

"We have to look though," said Holly.

"I'm not sure I feel very brave," said Puck in a small voice, "now I don't have any magic." He began backing away from the edge as he spoke – then stopped and shook himself. "But I have to help my mom," he said under his breath. He looked determinedly at the Pony Pools. "Okay," he said at last. "Let's investigate."

"We can go in together," said Holly, reaching out to stroke his mane, wanting to give him courage.

They entered the warm water side by side, splashing through the gentle waves until the ground began to slip away from them.

Puck and Holly turned to look at each other.
"Time to go under the water," said Puck
bravely. They each took a deep breath and
dove into the crystal depths.

Everything was so clear. Holly could see all
the way to the bottom, where the sand
sparkled like a golden carpet and

anemones clung to coral caves, waving their pink and purple fronds. Further ahead, a large black rock lay at the deepest point of the pool, gleaming darkly. Holly thought she could see the water swirling around it and was about to dive down to investigate, when she realized she needed more air.

She looked over at Puck, signaling that she was going to swim back to the surface.

As she turned though, she felt a sudden surge of current pulling her down. Holly struggled against it, growing more and more frantic as she sensed its strength. However hard she tried, she seemed to be sliding deeper and deeper into the pool. She looked around for Puck and saw by his frightened eyes and waving hoofs that he was being sucked down too. He nodded over to the black rock, and there, rising up behind it, Holly saw a swirling whirlpool of darker water, spreading from the depths like an evil wraith –
and wrapping itself around them.

Holly made one last desperate push for the surface but the strange whirlpool had her in its grip. She tumbled over and over, spiraling down at incredible speed into a tunnel of murky green water.

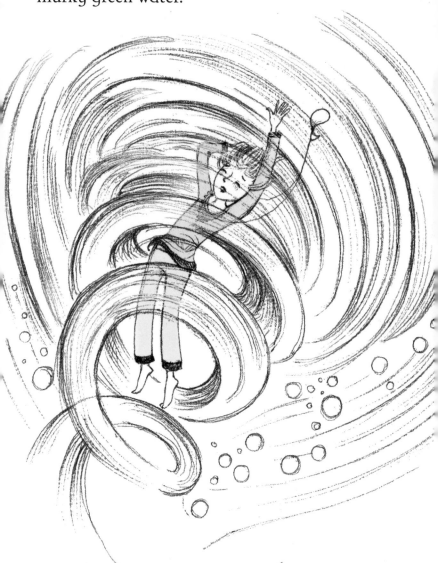

Chapter Three

Holly shut her eyes. She had no idea where the whirling water was taking her, only that there was nothing she could do to fight it. But after a few moments, the downward pull of the current changed and she felt herself being pushed to the surface once more. She opened her eyes just as she and Puck broke free of the water out into the fresh air, gasping in deep breaths. Only then did she look around, and realize that they were no longer in the Pony Pools.

Around them were twisting trees and melting shadows. The water here was thick and sludgy, coating their skin in a strange slime. Together they swam to the edge of the pool, hauling themselves out of the murky depths.

"I don't understand," said Holly, still panting for breath. "Where are we?" The thickly knotted branches blocked out most of the light and a foul smell hung in the air, dank and heavy. "And how did we get here?"

"I don't know," said Puck. "I've never been here before. The only place I can think this might be is the Dark Forest – nowhere else on Pony Island could be as dark and creepy as this."

They stood still for a moment in the eerie silence, which was unbroken by birdsong or even the sound of the wind.

Then they heard voices, low and rumbling, drawing closer and closer. Without a word, Puck and Holly searched for a hiding place, ducking down among the tangled undergrowth. Peering out through the thorny bushes, they could just make out three huge, dark ponies coming toward the pool. One had a white star on his forehead, one had a long dark tail which whipped the ground menacingly, and the last, and largest, had powerful glittering wings.

"Shadow, Storm and Ravenstar!" gasped Puck. "I thought they were finished with their plotting! What are those evil ponies up to now?"

Holly froze as Shadow approached the pool. He bent over it, staring into its gloomy depths. "I've perfected this spell now. I've used it again and again these last two days and it's never failed me. And still the fairy ponies haven't figured it out! Would you like to see the magic at work?"

Storm and Ravenstar nodded, and Shadow began to chant a spell.

"Ancient legend of long ago
Once again let your magic flow.
Open the link from waters here
To Pony Pools, so crystal clear.
A link that has been hidden well
Open now to my potent spell!"

As Shadow spoke, the green waters of the pool cleared, leaving it a glassy blue.

"Look!" whispered Holly. "I can see the Pony Pools reflected in the water. The image is so clear – it's like looking in a mirror."

"I think I know what this is!" Puck whispered back. "It must be the Enchanted Pool. There's a legend that says there's a magical mirror pool hidden somewhere on the island. It's connected to the Pony Pools by a secret tunnel and when you look through it, you can see what's happening in the pools. But I still don't understand what Shadow's using it for…"

He broke off as Storm and Ravenstar stepped toward Shadow, staring intently into the Enchanted Pool. Puck and Holly leaned further out of the bushes to peer into the water too.

Holly gasped at what she saw. There
was the Pony Queen, about to step into the
Magic Pony Pools, her creamy, buttermilk
coat gleaming in the sunshine. Around her was
a golden glow, flickering like a magical halo.

A cruel smile hovered over Shadow's lips as
he watched her. "Ha ha!" he said.

"Royal Bathing Time – just as I thought.
Now I can complete my plan."

Then he chanted another spell:

"Seize the magic from the Queen in the pool
Send it through the waters clear, deep and cool.
This is my time, my moment, my hour
Let me steal away her strength and power."

Holly watched, amazed, as the spell
began to work its magic. The golden
halo around the Pony Queen lifted, then
swirled through the waters of the Pony
Pools. It was as if the Queen's golden magic
was being sucked away by an invisible force,
while she smiled and bathed, unaware
anything was happening.

The golden glow began to fill the
Enchanted Pool, shimmering on its surface
like a sparkling mist, blotting out the
reflection of the Magic Pony Pools. Shadow
gave a crow of delight, then bent down to
drink the water.

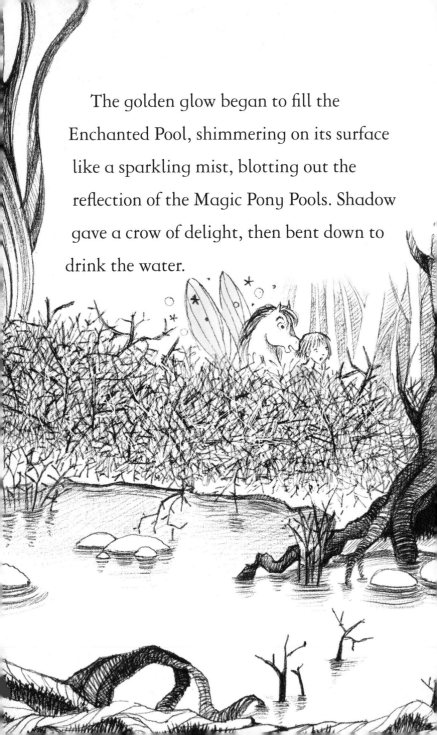

As he drank, the glow
began to sparkle around him like
a starlit cloak, beautiful and dazzling.

Puck and Holly looked at each
other in horror.

"Holly," Puck whispered, "I think Shadow is stealing the fairy ponies' magic through the pools."

"I know—" Holly began, then stopped as Shadow began speaking again.

"Now I have the Pony Queen's power," he boasted to his henchmen, "no pony will be able to stand up to me. I am the most magical pony on the island!"

Puck made as if to move forward, his brow furrowed in anger, but Holly held him back.

"Without her magic, the Pony Queen will be easier to overcome than a newborn foal. Storm, Ravenstar, follow me to the Summer Palace. It's time for me to claim her crown."

Chapter Four

Puck and Holly rushed out from their hiding place as Shadow and his henchmen galloped into the distance.

"What are we going to do?" cried Holly. "We have to stop Shadow! But he's so powerful…"

"We have to do more than that," Puck replied. "We need to save my mom, the Pony

Queen – and Pony Island. It's up to us now."

"Okay," said Holly, taking a deep breath. "Let's fly to the Summer Palace. We have to at least warn the Pony Queen of Shadow's plan and get the message out about the pools."

"You're forgetting – I can't fly," said Puck, shaking his head sorrowfully. "Shadow has stolen my powers too."

Holly tried to swallow down a surge of panic as she realized how little chance they stood of overcoming Shadow. Without Puck's magic, how could they ever hope to save the ponies?

"There must be something we can think of though…" Puck said mournfully.

Suddenly, Holly gasped. "I think I have the answer!" she cried. She pointed to the Enchanted Pool. There, hovering above its surface, was a faint golden mist. "Look!" she said excitedly. "There's still some of the Pony Queen's magic left in the pool. If you drink from it, Puck, you might be able to regain some powers."

Puck's eyes lit up. He ran over to the pool, gazing at the pulsing glow on its surface, then bent to drink. Holly watched in wonder as she saw the glow lift from the pool, just as it had with Shadow, and surround Puck like a golden cloak.

Puck drank all he could, and when at last he raised his head, his eyes were shining. "I can feel it!" he cried. "My magic has come back."

He fluttered his butterfly wings and rose effortlessly from the ground. "And I can fly again!"

Holly rushed over to him, ready to leave for the palace, but Puck was still staring at the Enchanted Pool. "I think there's still a little magic left in the water, Holly. I can see it. Why don't you drink some too? You might gain some powers that could help us fight against Shadow. And we need all the help we can get."

Holly hesitated only for a moment. She had no idea what might happen if she drank the water… But she had to do it, for the sake of the ponies. She kneeled by the pool and cupped her hands, lifting the glowing water to her lips. It tasted fresh and cool, but as she drank it she felt a faint tingling all over her body. Holly kept drinking until the last of the golden sparkles had disappeared.

"I think it's worked," said Puck excitedly. "I can see some sparkles around you too."

"Well, I definitely can't fly," said Holly, flapping her arms.

Puck laughed. "But you might be able to cast spells. Don't try any now – we don't want to use up your magic. Quick, let's get to the palace as fast as we can!"

Holly leaped onto Puck's back and they galloped through the dense forest.

Holly longed to be free of the gnarled, twisting trees, and take to the air. The trees seemed to crowd around them, blocking them in. Puck stumbled over roots and Holly was forced to push away sweeping branches, but they didn't stop. Despite the speed of the gallop, both Puck and Holly were shivering as they neared the forest's edge, its cold, dank air seeping under their skin.

But at last the trees began to thin. Puck stretched out his wings and leaped into the air, flying as fast as he could.

"We'll be too late to stop Shadow," said Holly, as the ground swept by beneath them and the palace's gleaming turrets came into view. "He must have reached the Pony Queen by now."

Puck said nothing as he landed on the palace lawn, fluttering down silently on the lush green grass, but his jaw was set with determination.

"What happens if we see Shadow?" Holly asked, slipping from Puck's back as she spoke. "His powers are still far greater than ours."

"We'll find a way to stand up to him," said Puck.

They looked at each other, giving brief smiles, then strode into the palace together.

All was ominously quiet. The palace guards were nowhere to be seen, nor were any other fairy ponies. Puck's hoofs made soft tapping noises on the marble floors, and he and Holly kept glancing around, expecting to catch sight of Shadow at any moment.

There was no sign of him. But as they reached the Pony Queen's chambers, they came upon a group of glittering statues.

"The Spell-Keepers!" gasped Puck.

"What's Shadow done to them?"

Holly rushed up to the statues, putting out her hands to touch them, then gasping in horror. The Spell-Keepers were icy cold – her warm breath cast a misty sheen on their frozen bodies. "They've been turned to ice," she whispered. Apart from their eerie stillness and ice-cold skin, they looked the same as ever, but their eyes were unseeing, blank and glazed. Among the statues was Bluebell, Puck's mother. Holly saw Puck nuzzle her neck, tears in his eyes.

Then, from inside the chamber, they heard the low, ringing tones of Shadow's voice. Puck and Holly crept around the icy statues toward the door. Through a crack in the door, they caught a glimpse of Shadow and Storm hovering menancingly above the Pony Queen, while Ravenstar blocked the door.

"You've lost your powers. Now give up your throne," Shadow demanded. "I want you to call a meeting for all fairy ponies. Then, in front of everyone, you will give me your crown so they know I am their new leader."

"Never," said the Pony Queen. "You may have stolen my magic but you have no right to rule, and I will not give up my crown."

"Then you leave me with no choice," snarled Shadow. And he began to chant.

"Grow weaker, and weaker still,
As you near death's lonely chill.
Now your life force drains away,
You are Queen and you must pay."

Puck and Holly watched in horror as the Pony Queen began to grow weak and pale. Her creamy coat turned a ghostly white, her dark eyes now seeming huge in her blanched face.

"I can't bear it," gasped Puck. "Unless we stop Shadow…the Pony Queen is going to die…"

"I'll leave you now," Shadow went on, smiling as he watched the Pony Queen crumple to the floor. "We're going down to the palace dungeons – to set up my headquarters there. But I'll return in an hour. If you agree to give up the throne, I'll reverse the spell. If not, the spell will work its magic…until you are no more!"

Chapter Five

Holly and Puck hid behind the icy statues as Shadow, Storm and Ravenstar left the chamber and charged past them. Holly could see Puck trembling and she looked down at her own hands to realize they were shaking too. Together, they walked up to the Pony Queen.

"Your Majesty!" said Holly, kneeling beside

her. "We saw what happened. There must be a way we can save you."

"We can't let Shadow take over Pony Island," Puck added. "Tell us what to do — we'll do anything."

The Pony Queen tried to say something, but it only came out as a faint whisper. Puck bent closer still, desperately trying to catch her words.

Holly watched him as he strained to make out what the Pony Queen was saying. He looked puzzled at first, but then his brow cleared and a look of amazement came over his face.

"The banishment spell!" he gasped. "Of course…"

"What is it?" asked Holly.

Puck turned to her excitedly. "It's an incredibly powerful spell that can only be used once, on the orders of the Pony Queen. It banishes evil from the island. All the ponies learn it at Pony Magic School – but I don't know if we can do it in time…or if we have the strength to make it work."

"Why not?" asked Holly. "Do you need to prepare for it?"

"It's not that," Puck explained. "The spell only works if it's said by a huge gathering of fairy ponies. They have to bring their powers together. That's what makes it so powerful — and so difficult to do."

"Then what are we waiting for?" asked Holly. "We must let everyone know. I'm sure we can make it work."

Puck looked doubtful. "But so many ponies have lost their magic," he said. "There may not be enough of us."

"We have to try," Holly insisted.

Puck nodded. "You're right. And it's our only chance."

"Let's ring the palace bell," said Holly. "Isn't that the best way to summon the ponies?"

Puck shook his head. "Shadow's still in the

palace, remember. If he finds out what we're up to, he'll stop it at once. We have to try and do it without him realizing." He paused for a moment, frowning in concentration. "I know – we'll write a message in the sky. While he's in the dungeons, there's no chance he'll see it."

Puck turned back to the Pony Queen. "We'll leave now, Your Majesty. We'll do our best."

With a great effort, the Pony Queen raised her eyes to theirs, as if in that glance she was trying to give them courage. Then she looked meaningfully toward the large open window in her chamber wall.

"Of course!" said Holly. "We'll leave through the window. That way, there's less chance Shadow will see us."

With her heart beating fast at the thought

of what lay before them, Holly leaped onto Puck's back and he took flight through the open window, beating his butterfly wings with powerful up-thrusts until they were soaring high above the palace.

"We'll write the sky message above the Singing River," said Puck. "That's the most central point on the island. If I chant the spell, will you try to use your magic to write the message? I've never done a sky message before. I'm not sure I'll be able to say the spell and write at the same time…" His voice trailed off doubtfully.

"Of course," said Holly, trying to put a confidence in her voice that she didn't feel. She was terrified to think that it was up to her and Puck to save Pony Island – and she wasn't even sure that the magic would work for her at all.

Puck whispered the message in Holly's ear as he circled in the sky above the Singing River. Then he began the Sky Spell.

"I write a message in the sky
A trail behind me as I fly.
Show ponies everywhere our plea,
Blazing brightly for all to see."

"Now, Holly!" cried Puck. "Reach out with your finger. Let the magic flow through your veins…and write the message."

Holly stretched out her hand, hoping that something would happen. With a gasp of delight, she felt the magic tingling down her arm and, as Puck flew, she was able to write a great, looping message in the air.

The words slipped from her fingertip in a sparkling trail, glowing like a firework in the sky.

Fairy Ponies everywhere come to the palace immediately to save the Pony Queen

When it was done, Puck began spiraling back down to the ground, landing at the edge of the palace gardens, along the banks of the Singing River. Behind them, the Summer Palace nestled in the folds of the Forever Flower Meadow, seemingly peaceful in the warm glow of the late afternoon light. Holly gazed at the palace for a moment, struck by the thought of the Pony Queen lying inside, her life ebbing away under Shadow's evil spell.

"We're doing all we can to help," said Puck, seeing the fear on Holly's face. "This has to work, for the Pony Queen and my mom. Come on – I'll teach you the banishment spell while we wait for the other fairy ponies."

Holly tried to keep her thoughts fixed on the spell, but she kept worrying about Shadow.

They only had an hour…would all the ponies
come in time?

"Look!" Puck said suddenly. And Holly
glanced up to see the sky filling with fairy

ponies, their tails streaming behind them,
their butterfly wings shining as they caught
the sun.

The ponies came from Sunlit Sea and

Rainbow Shore – there were even unicorns from the Enchanted Woods. Those that had lost their powers galloped over the grassy hills.

"And there's Izagard!" Holly cried excitedly, as the old wizard pony swooped down from the High Mountains.

"They're coming from all over the island," added Puck in amazement.

"I can't believe it's working," said Holly. "Oh, Puck!" she exclaimed. "The River Ponies are coming too."

One by one the River Ponies were emerging

from the waters of the Singing River, their
heads rising above the surface,
their bodies glistening
like ocean pearls.

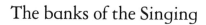

*Maybe we will be able
to do it after all,* Holly
thought.

The banks of the Singing
River were soon crowded with fairy ponies as
more and more came to join them, galloping
across the meadows at full speed, their bodies
cutting a swathe through the wildflowers.

Puck fluttered into the air above them all,
Holly on his back. He took a deep breath
before he spoke, trying to compose himself,
aware that all the fairy ponies were
watching him.

"Welcome all, and thank you for coming," he began. "We have some terrible news. It is Shadow who has been stealing your powers. And now he has taken the Pony Queen's too. He has cast a terrible spell, threatening her life unless she gives up the throne."

The fairy ponies began muttering amongst themselves and Holly glimpsed rows of shocked and horrified faces.

"The Pony Queen has asked us to come

together to cast the banishment spell," Puck

went on. "I know it can only ever be used

once, but I think now is the time. It's our only

hope of saving the Pony Queen."

All the fairy ponies nodded their heads

and stamped their hoofs to show

they were ready.

"Will our magic be enough?" an old pony spoke up. "So many of us have lost our powers."

"Could everyone who still has their magic please come forward?" asked Holly.

There was a brief jostling as ponies from the back made their way forward. But as the fairy ponies gathered into their two groups, there were gasps from the crowd.

"I didn't realize that so many had lost their magic," Holly murmured.

"Most ponies go to the Magic Pony Pools every morning…" said Puck, voicing his thoughts. "Maybe we're lucky so many of us still have our powers."

"But can we defeat Shadow?" asked Holly.

"I don't know," Puck whispered in reply.

He opened his mouth to ask everyone to

chant the spell together, but before he could speak, the palace bells began to peal.

Everyone turned to look as the doors of the Summer Palace were flung open, and Shadow strode out to face them. On his head, he wore a gleaming crown.

"Oh no!" cried Holly. "It's too late. We've run out of time!"

Chapter Six

Behind Shadow came Storm and Ravenstar. Holly could just make out the Pony Queen, carried on a roughly-made stretcher across their backs. She lay horribly still, blinking feebly in the last rays of the setting sun.

"I am your king now!" Shadow declared. "I am leader of Pony Island. Look at your Pony Queen. She can't even lift her head. She has been defeated and soon she will fade away."

As he spoke, he spun around, casting a spell on the Summer Palace. There was a flash of light followed by a foul stench that lingered in the air. Holly shielded her eyes against the glare, and when she looked up again she saw black roses had covered the palace.

Their huge thorns protruded like vicious prongs, as if to ward off anyone who might dare enter.

Shadow let out a low cackle. "That is just a small sign of my power – and of things to come," he told the fairy ponies. "You have no choice but to obey me. You are mine to control."

"We'll never accept you as our king," shouted Puck.

The ponies cheered in agreement, and before Shadow could react, Holly called down to them all. "Now!" she cried. "It's time to say the spell."

Together, Puck and Holly began to chant the banishment spell. The other fairy ponies quickly joined in, until their voices made up a chorus, from Izagard's deep boom to the lilting tones of the River Ponies. The sound filled the valley, echoing off the distant slopes of the High Mountains.

"We chant together, voices loud,
We summon winds and swirling cloud,
A spell from early mists of time,
To banish evil and vile crime.
Our voices raised in chanting song,
Joined together to make us strong."

As Holly said the words, she could feel her body tingling and fizzing again, and her voice took on a power and depth it had never had before — the magic from the pools was still with her. It was amazing to hear her voice mingling

with those of all the other fairy ponies, as they
said the spell over and over again. The fairy
ponies stamped their hoofs as they chanted,
until the ground shook beneath them, and they
moved steadily forward. They advanced on
Shadow, summoning courage with their
pounding strides.

At first, Shadow's expression didn't change.
He stood in front of the thorny palace,

his face triumphant, as if he believed that nothing could ever harm him thanks to his newfound powers. But then, in the distance, Holly saw a great shimmering cloud begin to form. It swirled through the air, growing larger all the time, glittering with sparkling dust, golden and potent.

"A magic tornado," gasped Puck, watching in awe as it swept over the Singing River, heading straight for Shadow, Storm and Ravenstar.

Shadow's henchmen turned and fled in fear, heading toward the river. But it was as if the swirling cloud had a mind of its own, pushing them toward the gathered ponies. They rushed back to cower behind Shadow.

"You fools!" said Shadow, snarling at them. "I can easily control this."

He cast a spell, summoning the power of a storm, then blew at the cloud. Holly could see his breath on the air like a silver mist. It started out as a thin wisp, then billowed out into a giant cloud filled with icy crystals, sparkling like a thousand daggers.

Holly felt herself tense as she watched the two clouds meet, the icy wind from Shadow's storm cloud blowing against her, chilling and frightening.

For a moment, the fairy ponies left off their chanting as they gazed at the battle of the winds. The golden tornado twisted around Shadow's storm cloud, only to be blown back again.

"We must keep saying the spell to keep it strong," Puck shouted above the howling winds.

They began chanting again, and Holly watched as, this time, their swirling tornado whipped away Shadow's storm cloud, scattering it like spray from the sea. Then the tornado funneled down from the sky, aiming straight for Shadow and his henchmen.

"It's working!" she cried excitedly. "We're beating Shadow together."

For the first time, Shadow lost his arrogant stare. He cast spell after spell at the tornado, now desperate to make it stop. He pelted it with thunderbolts, then breathed fire like a dragon, as if trying to burn the cloud away. But all his efforts were in vain.

He snorted furiously. "Fly!" he shouted at Storm and Ravenstar.

The three ponies took to the sky, but the tornado swooped after them, its long tendrils sweeping around them, cutting off any chance of escape. They landed clumsily and huddled by the doors of the palace as the cloud bore down upon them. Then, in one

swift motion, it plucked them from the
ground, as if they were no more than seeds on
the wind.

The fairy ponies stopped chanting and gazed in amazement as the cloud carried Storm, Shadow and Ravenstar away, swirling them through the air until they were faint specks on the horizon.

Holly threw her arms around Puck. "We've done it!" she said. "We've really done it."

All around them, the fairy ponies began to cheer. "Long live the Pony Queen!" they cried.

But the Pony Queen didn't move. She lay on the banks of the Singing River, where Storm and Ravenstar had left her.

Chapter Seven

The Pony Queen was still breathing but only feebly. Her eyelashes fluttered gently, but she made no other movement.

Holly felt a surge of panic. "I thought if we banished Shadow, the Pony Queen would recover."

"So did I!" Puck replied.

Holly rushed forward, Puck at her side.

"Your Majesty, what can we do to save you?" she asked. But there was no reply.

Holly fell to her knees, unable to restrain herself. She wrapped her arms around the Pony Queen and began to cry, tears sliding down her face, falling in drops onto the pale coat of the silent Queen.

She heard Puck's sudden intake of breath, but didn't look up, instead burying her face in the Pony Queen's mane, which was soon wet with her tears. But then Holly felt the Pony Queen stir beneath her, and she loosened her hold. She fell back, watching in amazement. The Pony Queen's sparkle and glow was starting to return, the lank hair of her mane and tail becoming thick and lustrous...until at last she raised herself from the ground, shaking her head, her eyes sparkling and full of life. She looked more dazzling than ever as she fluttered her shimmering wings, rising into the air so that all the fairy ponies could see that her life force had returned.

"What happened?" asked Holly, her words coming out in an astonished whisper. "I don't understand..."

The Pony Queen laughed. "I don't understand it either, Holly," she said. "But I am profoundly grateful to you."

"Did I save you somehow?" Holly asked. "Could it have been something to do with the magic I drank from the Enchanted Pool?"

She heard a gruff voice behind her, and turned to see the wise eyes of Izagard, the wizard pony, looking at her with respect. "There's an old legend that says if a fairy pony's life force is draining away, the only thing that can save it is the tears of a human child. I always thought it was just a legend, but perhaps, after all, it's true."

"We'll never know," said the Pony Queen, smiling at them both. "But whatever it was… thank you, Holly."

They looked up at the sound of whirring wings, and Holly could see the fairy ponies filling the air, Shadow's bind over them broken at last, their powers of flight returned.

"And look!" cried Holly. "The Spell-Keepers."

Puck leaped for joy as he saw his mother flying out of the palace and streaking across the sky. "You're safe," he said, as Bluebell swooped down beside him. "I was so worried when I found you frozen in the palace."

He nuzzled close to her, resting his head against her side.

The gathered ponies fell quiet as the Pony Queen rose above the crowd once more. "Shadow has been defeated," she declared. "It was thanks to you all, coming together to say the banishment spell, and to Puck and Holly, for acting so swiftly, and so bravely."

A cheer went up from the fairy ponies and Holly rushed over to hug Puck and Bluebell. She was bursting with happiness.

The Pony Queen fluttered down from the sky and came to rest on a grassy slope by the Singing River, the fairy ponies all crowding around her.

"I'll cast a special spell over the Enchanted Pool in the Dark Forest," she told them, "closing its link to the Magic Pony Pools, so that this can never happen again."

"But now," she went on, "it is time to celebrate. Everyone follow me."

The Pony Queen headed back into the palace, casting a spell as she flew. There was a flash of rainbow light and the piercing thorns and blackened roses vanished. In their place, the beautiful, pale pink roses returned, their sweet scent filling the warm evening air. Around the roses flitted clouds of fireflies, magically lighting up the walls of the palace like hundreds of tiny flames.

The fairy ponies flooded into the courtyard of the palace, where the Pony Queen's spell continued to weave its magic. The palace was strewn with banners, fireworks filled the sky

above the courtyard with all the colors of the
rainbow, and tinkling fountains made music
as they flowed. Soon the palace was filled
with happy chatter, as the fairy
ponies mingled and laughed.
They feasted on delicious
fairy cakes, honeydew juice
and flower blossom sorbets
from heavily laden tables.

As the Fairy Pony band
began to play, Holly felt

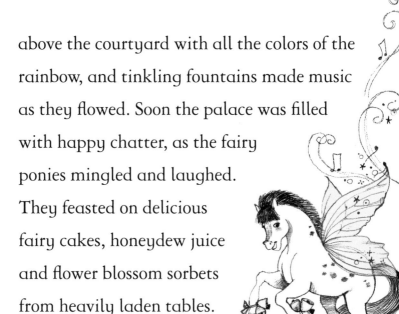

her eyes grow heavy with tiredness.

"Puck," she said after a while,
"I think it's time I went
back to the Great Oak.
Will you
take me?"

"Of course," said Puck. "But first let's say goodbye to the Pony Queen."

Together they made their way over to her.

"Are you leaving us, Holly?" asked the Pony Queen, smiling at them.

Holly nodded. "But I hope I can come back again soon."

"You are always welcome here," replied the Pony Queen. "After all, we could never have defeated Shadow without you."

"Oh! Do you think I have any magic left?" Holly asked, suddenly remembering how amazing it had felt to write the sky message and chant the banishment spell.

But the Pony Queen shook her head. "When Shadow was banished, all the magic was returned to the ponies it came from. But

you don't need magic, Holly," she added.
"Thanks to you, we are all safe now."

Holly reached up to hug the Pony Queen
goodbye, then she and Puck slipped through
the crowded palace and out into the fresh
night air. Above them, the stars twinkled down
from the inky black sky, and the moon shone
brightly over Pony Island. Holly climbed onto
Puck's back and he took to the skies.

Wrapping her arms around Puck's neck,
Holly gazed down at the Singing River,
winding its way like a silver thread across the
island. The valleys lay like shadowy folds
between the hills, and the wildflowers were
hidden under the cover of darkness, only their
sweet scent rising up on the summer air. Puck
and Holly flew in silence, happy in each

other's company. Holly drank in the view, knowing it might be a while before she could visit Pony Island again. *I helped save the Pony Queen!* she thought to herself as they flew. Although she was leaving Pony Island, she felt overjoyed that Shadow had been banished forever.

At last, they came to the entrance to the Great Oak and as Puck set her down, Holly gave him one last hug.

"Promise you'll come back," said Puck.

Holly nodded. "I'll visit Great-Aunt May again as soon as I can."

"And then we'll have more amazing adventures on Pony Island," said Puck, nuzzling her shoulder.

With a last stroke of his mane, Holly

turned and wandered slowly down the secret
tunnel in the oak tree. She kept glancing back
over her shoulder, to catch one last glimpse of
Pony Island. Puck stayed at the entrance,
watching her until she gave a last wave. "I
promise I'll come to Pony Island again," she
whispered to herself. "It's the most magical
place in the world."

Enter the world of the

Fairy Ponies

and collect every enchanting tale

For more Fairy Ponies titles
visit our website at

www.edcpub.com or
www.usbornebooksandmore.com

Edited by Stephanie King and Becky Walker

Designed by Brenda Cole

Additional design by Elisabetta Barbazza

Reading consultant: Alison Kelly,
University of Roehampton

First published in 2014 by Usborne Publishing Ltd.,
Usborne House, 83-85 Saffron Hill, London EC1N 8RT, England.
www.usborne.com

Copyright © Usborne Publishing, 2014

Illustrations copyright © Usborne Publishing, 2014

Cover and inside illustrations by Barbara Bongini

The name Usborne and the devices 🔱 👑 are Trade Marks of
Usborne Publishing Ltd.

A CIP catalogue record for this book is available from the British Library.

This edition published in America in 2015 AE.

PB ISBN 9780794535537   ALB ISBN 9781601303837

JFMAMJJA OND/15   02354/4

Printed in Dongguan, Guangdong, China.